I AM A DROID

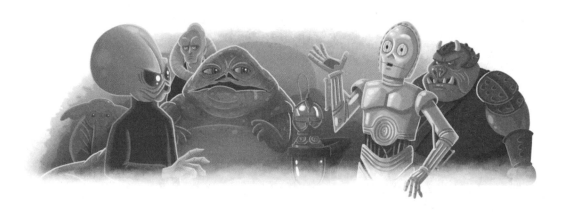

By Christopher Nicholas
Illustrated by Chris Kennett

 A GOLDEN BOOK • NEW YORK

© & ™ 2016 LUCASFILM LTD. All rights reserved. Published in the United States by Golden Books, an imprint of Random House Children's Books, a division of Penguin Random House LLC, 1745 Broadway, New York, NY 10019, and in Canada by Random House of Canada, a division of Penguin Random House Ltd., Toronto. Golden Books, A Golden Book, A Little Golden Book, the G colophon, and the distinctive gold spine are registered trademarks of Penguin Random House LLC.
randomhousekids.com
ISBN 978-0-7364-3489-8 (trade) — ISBN 978-0-7364-3490-4 (ebook)
Printed in the United States of America
10 9 8 7 6 5 4 3 2 1

I am a droid.

I am built to do a special job.

Some droids are **small**.

Some droids are

BIG.

Some

droids

walk...

 some droids **roll**...

and some droids fly!

Astromech droids like R2-D2 repair starships and starfighters.

Beep-bop-boop!

They also help pilots navigate a course through the **stars**.

Protocol droids like C-3PO are programmed to understand millions of different languages.

They help aliens from strange planets talk to each other.

Some droids are built to fight!
Battle droids, **super battle droids**,
and **destroyer droids** help armies
win battles.

Zap! Zap!

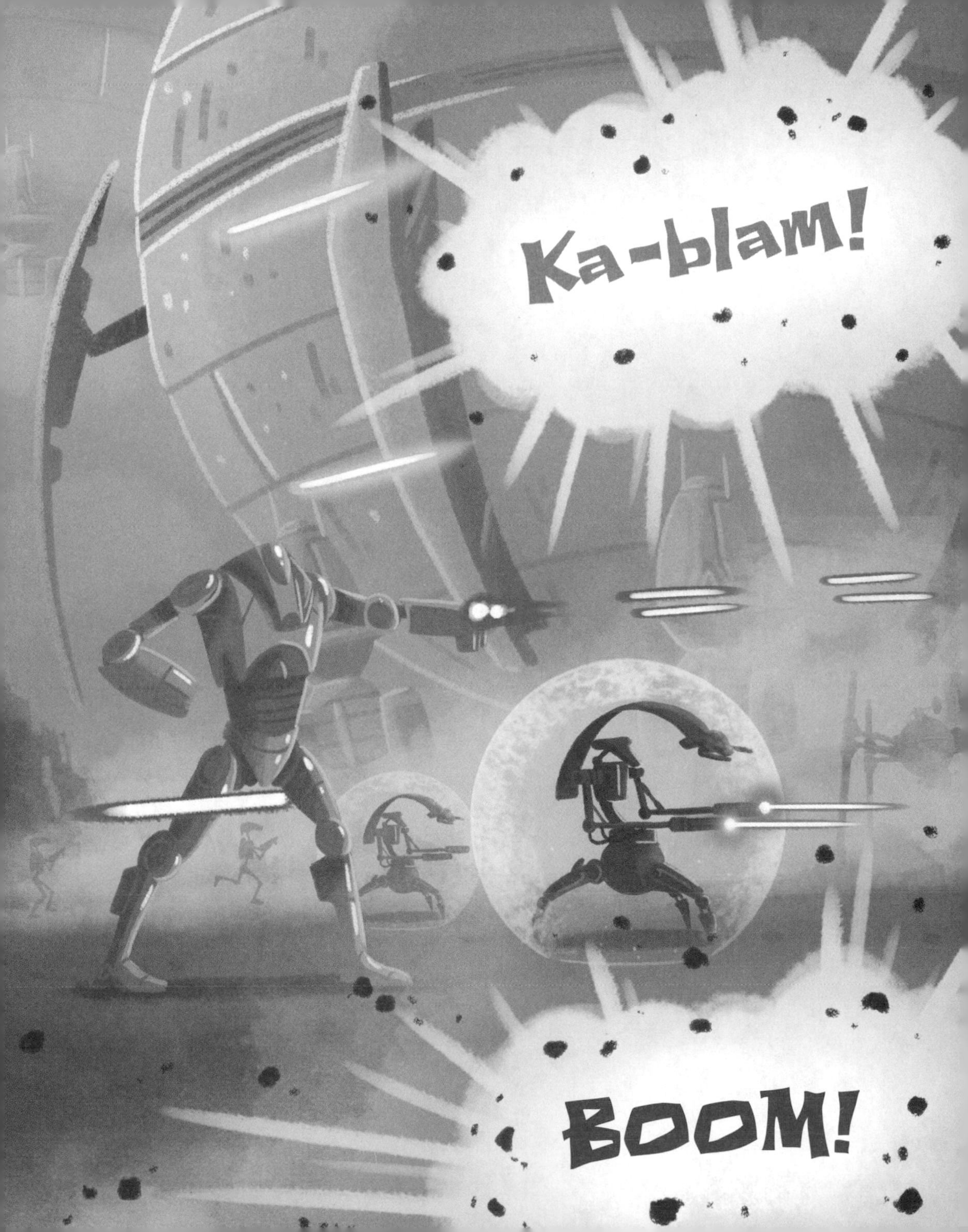
Ka-blam!
BOOM!

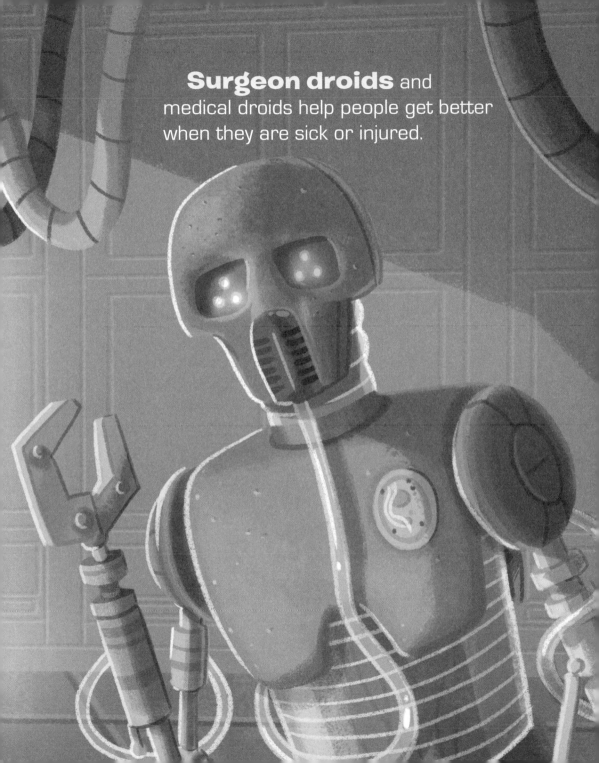

Surgeon droids and medical droids help people get better when they are sick or injured.

Some droids are **bounty hunters**.
IG-88 and 4-LOM track down humans and
aliens who are on the run.

Probe droids are spies!

They report **secret** information to their masters.

Some droids are built to protect.
MagnaGuard droids help keep
General Grievous safe from his enemies.

Power droids are like big walking batteries!

Some droids aren't very nice.

But some droids are **heroes**!